36205

.CLASSICS.
Illustrated.®

Mark Twain
HUCKLEBERRY FINN

essay by

Andrew J. Hoffman, Ph.D.
Brown University

ACCLAIM BOOKS

STUDY GUIDE

Adventures of Huckleberry Finn

art by Frank Giacoia

Classics Illustrated: Adventures of Huckleberry Finn
© Twin Circle Publishing Co.,
a division of Frawley Enterprises; licensed to First Classics, Inc.
All new material and compilation © 1997 by Acclaim Books, Inc.

Dale-Chall R.L.: 6.4

ISBN 1-57840-008-2

Acclaim Books, New York, NY
Printed in the United States

STUDY GUIDE

HUCKLEBERRY FINN

*I*T WAS ROUGH LIVING IN A HOUSE ALL THE TIME, WEARING NEW CLOTHES, AND DOING LESSONS, ESPECIALLY SINCE I'D LIVED IN THE WOODS WITH PAP FOR SO LONG. BUT, WHEN HE DISAPPEARED, THE WIDOW DOUGLAS, SHE TOOK ME FOR HER SON AND ALLOWED SHE WOULD CIVILIZE ME.

SHE WAS DECENT ENOUGH, BUT HER OLD MAID SISTER, MISS WATSON, KEPT PECKING AT ME.

DON'T SCRUNCH UP LIKE THAT, HUCKLEBERRY FINN! PAY ATTENTION!

I DECLARE, SOMETIMES I THINK YOU'RE LAZY AND NO GOOD LIKE YOUR FATHER.

HUCK'S A POOR LOST LAMB, SISTER. I KNOW HE'S TRYING TO BEHAVE.

ONE NIGHT, WHEN I COULDN'T STAND IT AN LONGER.

ME-YOW.

ME-YOW.

I SLIPPED TO THE GROUND AND, SURE ENOUGH, THERE WAS TOM SAWYER.

C'MON. THE GANG IS WAITING.

NOW, WE'LL START THIS BAND OF ROBBERS AND CALL IT TOM SAWYER'S GANG.

WHAT'S THE LINE OF BUSINESS OF THIS GANG?

NOTHING, ONLY ROBBERY AND MURDER AND CATCHING SPIES AND AMBUSHING CARAVANS-- THINGS LIKE THAT.

WE GOT TO TAKE AN OATH NEVER TO TELL ANY OF THE SECRETS OF THE GANG. EVERY GANG THAT'S HIGH-TONED HAS ONE.

WHAT'S THE OATH?

IF ANYONE TELLS THE SECRETS, HE'LL BE KILLED, AND HIS FAMILY, TOO.

WHAT ABOUT HUCK? HE AIN'T GOT NO FAMILY EXCEPT HIS OLD DRUNK FATHER. AND *HE* AIN'T BEEN AROUND HERE FOR MORE THAN A YEAR.

BET HE AIN'T HEARD YOU GOT $6,000 FROM FINDING SOME STOLEN MONEY.

I RECKON NOT.

THEY WAS GOING TO RULE ME OUT BECAUSE EVERY BOY MUST HAVE A FAMILY OR SOMEBODY TO KILL OR IT WOULDN'T BE FAIR AND SQUARE FOR THE OTHERS. THEN...

HOW ABOUT MISS WATSON? YOU COULD KILL HER.

SHE'LL DO, HUCK. YOU CAN COME IN.

WELL, THREE OR FOUR MONTHS RUN ALONG AFTER THAT. I WENT TO SCHOOL AND COULD MULTIPLY UP TO SIX TIMES SEVEN IS THIRTY-FIVE, AND I DON'T RECKON I COULD GET ANY FURTHER THAN THAT IF I WAS TO LIVE FOREVER. THEN ONE MORNING...

FOOTPRINTS--WITH A CROSS IN THE LEFT BOOT HEEL.

I GOT TO GET ME TO JUDGE THATCHER'S.

THERE...

I WANT YOU TO TAKE ALL THE $6,000 YOU'RE KEEPING FOR ME--FOR A GIFT. I DON'T WANT IT NO MORE.

IS SOMETHING WRONG, HUCK?

JUST TAKE IT. PLEASE DON'T ASK ME NO QUESTIONS.

I THINK I UNDERSTAND. HERE, SIGN THIS PAPER. THAT WILL MAKE YOUR MONEY SAFE-- FROM ANYONE.

THAT NIGHT, I WENT HOME FEELING BETTER. I GOT TO MY ROOM, LIT THE CANDLE, AND...

PAP! I KNOWED IT WAS YOU WHEN I SAW THOSE TRACKS.

AIN'T YOU A SWEET-SCENTED DANDY, THOUGH? I BET I'LL TAKE SOME OF THOSE FRILLS OUT OF YOU.

THEY SAY YOU'RE RICH. GIT ME THAT $6,000.

I AIN'T GOT THE MONEY. ASK JUDGE THATCHER.

JUDGE THATCHER, EH? I'LL SHOW HIM WHO'S HUCK FINN'S BOSS. YOU COME WITH ME.

PAP TOOK ME FROM MISSOURI UP THE RIVER ABOUT THREE MILES TO THE ILLINOIS SHORE.

I GOT ME AN OLD LOG HUT WITH A GOOD STRONG LOCK ON THE DOOR. YOU'RE STAYIN' WITH ME NOW.

PAP KEPT ME WITH HIM ALL THE TIME. I GOT TO KIND OF LIKE THE LAZY LIFE AGAIN...

EXCEPT WHEN PAP GOT DRUNK AND OUT OF HIS HEAD.

YOU'RE THE ANGEL OF DEATH. I'LL KILL YOU!

PAP--IT'S ME--HUCK!

PRETTY SOON HE WAS ALL TIRED OUT.

I'LL REST A MINUTE AND GET STRONG AGAIN, AND THEN I'LL KILL YOU.

THEN HE DOZED OFF.

IT'S TIME I LIT OUT.

WHEN PAP WENT TO TOWN THE NEXT DAY, I GOT BUSY.

I SAWED A SECTION OF THE LOG OUT--BIG ENOUGH TO LET ME THROUGH.

AND THIS WILL LOOK LIKE THEY LIT OUT WITH THE SUPPLIES THIS WAY.

THEN...

I'LL HOLE UP ON JACKSON'S ISLAND FOR A SPELL. NOBODY EVER GOES THERE.

IT SURE IS GREAT TO LIE ON YOUR BACK IN THE MOONLIGHT AND NOT HAVE TO ANSWER TO NOBODY.

JACKSON'S ISLAND STOOD OUT IN THE MIDDLE OF THE MISSISSIPPI RIVER, BETWEEN MISSOURI AND ILLINOIS. IT DIDN'T TAKE ME TO LONG TO GET THERE.

THE NEXT MORNING...

IT WORKED! THEY'RE HUNTING FOR MY BODY. THE CANNON FIRED OVER THE WATER IS SUPPOSED TO MAKE MY CARCASS COME TO THE TOP.

THE FERRYBOAT COME IN PRETTY CLOSE. MOST EVERYBODY WAS ON IT

THERE'S PAP AND JUDGE THATCHER AND TOM SAWYER AND HIS AUNT POLLY AND THE WIDOW DOUGLAS AND MISS WATSON.

A WHILE LATER...

THEY'RE GIVING UP, NOW. I'M SAFE.

I MADE CAMP AND LAZED ABOUT THE ISLAND FOR THREE DAYS. THEN...

A FRESH CAMPFIRE! SOMEONE'S ON THIS ISLAND WITH ME!

I UNCOCKED MY GUN AND WENT SNEAKING BACK AS FAST AS I COULD.

I DIDN'T SLEEP MUCH THAT NIGHT.

I GOT TO FIND OUT WHO IT IS.

WHAT ARE YOU DOING HERE, JIM?

YOU WOULDN'T TELL ON ME, WOULD YOU, HUCK?

I RUN OFF!

MISS WATSON WAS GOIN' TO SELL ME DOWN TO NEW ORLEANS--SO I LIT OUT.

HOW LONG HAVE YOU BEEN ON THE ISLAND?

I COME HERE THE NIGHT AFTER YOU WAS KILLED.

WE DECIDED TO MAKE A GOOD CAMP. WE FOUND A BIG CAVERN IN THE ROCK, AND PUT ALL THE THINGS HANDY AT THE BACK OF IT.

GET EVERYTHIN' IN, HUCK. THOSE LITTLE BIRDS, FLYIN' THAT WAY SAY IT'S GOIN' TO RAIN.

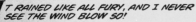

T RAINED LIKE ALL FURY, AND I NEVER SEE THE WIND BLOW SO!

THIS IS NICE. I WOULDN'T WANT TO BE NOWHERE ELSE.

THE RIVER ROSE FOR TEN OR TWELVE DAYS. ONE NIGHT...

CATCH ONTO THAT RAFT HUCK, MAYBE WE CAN USE IT.

ANOTHER NIGHT WE SAW A HOUSE THAT HAD BEEN CAUGHT UP IN THE FLOOD.

LET'S SEE WHAT'S INSIDE.

LOOK!

IT'S A DEAD MAN--SHOT IN THE BACK. DON'T LOOK, HUCK.

LET'S TAKE SOME OF THESE CLOTHES AND THINGS. THEY MIGHT COME IN HANDY.

WE GOT HOME ALL SAFE. A FEW DAYS LATER...

THINGS IS GETTING DULL. I'LL SLIP OVER TO TOWN AND FIND OUT WHAT'S GOING ON.

HERE'S A DRESS AND SUNBONNET WE GOT OFF THE FLOATIN' HOUSE. RECKON YOU'D BE SAFER IF YOU WENT AS A GIRL.

I GOT INTO ONE OF THE CALICO GOWNS.

HOW'S THIS?

IT'S A FAIR FIT...

...BUT QUIT PULLIN' UP YOUR SKIRT TO GET TO YOUR BRITCHES POCKET.

HAT NIGHT, IN TOWN...

WHO'S THERE?

SARAH WILLIAMS, MA'AM.

COME IN, CHILD. TAKE OFF YOUR BONNET.

NO, MA'AM. I'LL JUST REST AWHILE AND GO ON.

YOU SHOULDN'T BE OUT ALONE AT NIGHT. ILL HAVE MY HUSBAND GO ALONG WITH YOU AS SOON AS HE GETS BACK.

HE WENT WITH ANOTHER MAN TO SEE IF THEY COULD BORROW A BOAT. THEY'RE GOING OVER TO JACKSON'S ISLAND TONIGHT TO HUNT FOR A RUNAWAY SLAVE.

HIS NAME'S JIM, AND THEY SAY HE MURDERED HUCK FINN. THERE'S A $300 REWARD OUT FOR HIM.

WHY, HE...

WHAT DID YOU SAY YOUR NAME WAS, HONEY?

ER... MARY WILLIAMS.

I DOUBLED ON MY TRACKS AND SLIPPED BACK TO THE CANOE.

JUMPED IN AND DUG FOR OUR PLACE. THERE...

GET UP, JIM! THEY'RE AFTER US.

WE PUT EVERYTHING WE HAD IN THE WORLD ON OUR RAFT AND SLIPPED DOWN RIVER. THE NEXT DAY...

I RECKON IT'S SAFE TO STOP AND FIX UP THE RAFT SOME.

WE CAN MAKE A WIGWAM TO GET UNDER WHEN IT'S HOT OR RAINY, AND TO KEEP THE THINGS DRY.

LATER...

I JUDGE THAT WE'RE NOT FAR FROM CAIRO, AT THE BOTTOM OF ILLINOIS. WE CAN SELL THE RAFT THERE AND GET ON A STEAMBOAT AND GO UP THE OHIO RIVER AMONG THE FREE STATES.

IT MAKES ME TREMBLY AND FEVERISH ALL OVER TO BE SO NEAR TO FREEDOM.

THEN ONE NIGHT...

THE FOG'S TOO THICK TO RUN IN WITH THIS CURRENT. I'LL MAKE FAST A LINE TO THE SHORE.

BUT I LOST THE LINE. I SHOT OUT INTO THE SOLID FOG AND HADN'T NO MORE IDEA WHICH WAY I WAS GOING THAN A DEAD MAN.

JIM! JIM! WHERE ARE YOU?

I DIDN'T HEAR NOTHING.

I RECKON JIM AND THE RAFT ARE GONE FOREVER. I'LL JUST LIE DOWN HERE IN THE CANOE. I DON'T CARE WHAT HAPPENS TO ME.

YOU MUST'VE BEEN DREAMING.

I AIN'T NEVER HAD A DREAM BEFORE THAT'S TIRED ME LIKE THIS ONE.

AND HOW ABOUT THIS TRASH ON THE RAFT? THAT'S NO DREAM.

WHEN I LOSE YOU, MY HEART WAS MOST BROKE. AND WHEN I FIND YOU, THE TEARS COME, I'M SO THANKFUL. AND ALL YOU WAS THINKIN' ABOUT WAS HOW YOU COULD MAKE A FOOL OF OLD JIM.

HE GOT UP SLOW AND WALKED INTO THE WIGWAM.

JIM, I'M SORRY. IT WAS A MEAN TRICK.

THAT'S ALL RIGHT, HUCK. AIN'T YOU HELPING ME TO CAIRO AND FREEDOM?

WHEN I GETS THERE, I'LL BE SHOUTIN' FOR JOY AND IT'S ALL ON ACCOUNT OF HUCK. YOU IS THE BEST FRIEND JIM EVER HAD.

WE KEPT DRIFTING DOWN THE RIVER.

THAT'S CAIRO, HUCK. I JUST KNOWS IT.

I'LL TAKE THE CANOE AND SEE.

I HADN'T GOT FAR WHEN ALONG CAME A SKIFF.

WE'RE HUNTING FOR FIVE SLAVES THAT RUN OFF LAST NIGHT. ANY MEN ON YOUR RAFT?

JUST ONE-- MY PAP.

I RECKON WE'LL GO AND SEE FOR OURSELVES.

I WISH YOU WOULD. HE'S SICK, AND SO IS MAM AND MARY ANN.

BUT SHE COME SMASHING STRAIGHT THROUGH THE RAFT.

WHEN I BOUNCED TO THE TOP AGAIN...

JIM! JIM!

BUT I DIDN'T GET NO ANSWER.

I LIT OUT FOR SHORE, WHERE SOME PEOPLE TOOK ME IN. ONE DAY, ONE OF THEIR SLAVES CAME TO ME.

IF YOU'LL COME INTO THE SWAMP, I'LL SHOW YOU SOMETHIN' MIGHTY CURIOUS.

I FOLLOWED HIM AND...

JIM!

THAT'S RIGHT, HUCK!

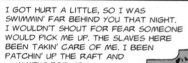

I GOT HURT A LITTLE, SO I WAS SWIMMIN' FAR BEHIND YOU THAT NIGHT. I WOULDN'T SHOUT FOR FEAR SOMEONE WOULD PICK ME UP. THE SLAVES HERE BEEN TAKIN' CARE OF ME. I BEEN PATCHIN' UP THE RAFT AND WAITIN' FOR YOU.

AS SOON AS IT WAS NIGHT, WE SHOVED OF

LET HER GO, JIM. HEAD FOR THE BIG WATER. WE'RE ON OUR WAY AGAIN.

A FEW DAYS LATER, I WAS PADDLING NEAR SHORE WHEN...

PLEASE TAKE US ABOARD, THE MEN AND DOGS ARE AFTER US.

C'MON IN.

I LIT OUT FOR THE RAFT AND THEY WERE SAFE. THEN...

WHAT GOT YOU INTO TROUBLE?

I'D BEEN SELLING AN ARTICLE TO TAKE THE TARTAR OFF OF TEETH. THE TARTAR CAME OFF ALL RIGHT...

...BUT SO DID THE ENAMEL.

I WAS SLIDING OUT OF TOWN WHEN I MET YOU. WHAT GOT THE DOGS ON YOU?

I BEEN RUNNIN' A LITTLE TEMPERANCE REVIVAL AND DOIN' VERY WELL UNTIL WORD GOT AROUND THAT I WAS DRINKIN' ON THE SLY.

NOBODY SAID ANYTHING FOR AWHILE, THEN ...

ALAS!

WHAT'RE YOU ALASSIN' ABOUT?

TO THINK THAT I, A DUKE, SHOULD BE IN SUCH COMPANY.

NO!

YES! I AM THE RIGHTFUL DUKE OF BRIDGEWATER, NOW DEGRADED TO THE COMPANIONSHIP OF FELONS ON A RAFT.

I'M SORRY FOR YOU, BILGEWATER, BUT YOU AIN'T THE ONLY PERSON THAT'S HAD TROUBLES LIKE THAT.

I--I'M THE LATE DAUPHIN-- SON OF LOOY THE SIXTEEN AND MARRY ANTONETTE.

AT YOUR AGE? NO! YOU MEAN YOU'RE THE LATE CHARLEMAGNE. YOU MUST BE 600 YEARS OLD, AT THE VERY LEAST!

ROUBLE HAS DONE IT, BILGEWATER. TROUBLE HAS BRUNG THESE GRAY HAIRS AND THIS PREMATURE BALDITUDE.

YES, GENTLEMEN, YOU SEE BEFORE YOU THE WANDERIN', EXILED, SUFFERIN' RIGHTFUL KING OF FRANCE.

IT DIDN'T TAKE ME LONG TO MAKE UP MY MIND THAT THESE LIARS WEREN'T NO KINGS NOR DUKES AT ALL, BUT JUST LOW-DOWN HUMBUGS AND FRAUDS. BUT I NEVER LET ON.

THEN THE KING, HE GETS NOSEY.

HE AIN'T A RUNAWAY SLAVE, IS HE?

GOODNESS, NO. BUT PEOPLE DO THINK THAT AND TRY TO TAKE HIM AWAY FROM ME. THAT'S WHY WE DON'T RUN DAYTIMES.

I'LL FIGURE OUT A WAY SO WE CAN RUN IN THE DAYTIME.

THEY DRESSED JIM IN THE DUKE'S KING LEAR OUTFIT.

THAT SHOULD KEEP PEOPLE AWAY.

SICK ARAB
BUT HARMLESS WHEN NOT OUT OF HIS HEAD.

THEN THEY STARTED MAKING PLANS.

HAVE YOU EVER TROD THE BOARDS, ROYALTY?

PLAYACTIN'? NO, BUT I'M FOR ANYTHIN' THAT WILL PAY.

THE NEXT TOWN WE COME TO, WE'LL HIRE A HALL AND DO ROMEO AND JULIET. I'LL LEARN YOU THE PART.

LATER...

DON'T YOU THINK MY WHITE WHISKERS IS GOIN' TO LOOK UNCOMMON ODD ON JULIET?

DON'T WORRY. THESE COUNTRY JAKES WON'T EVER THINK OF THAT.

I'M SO GLAD TO SEE MY OWN DEAR NEPHEW. HOW'S THE FAMILY? TELL ME ALL ABOUT THEM.

WHY, ER, YOU SEE...

CHILDREN, COME SAY HELLO TO YOUR COUSIN TOM..TOM SAWYER.

I ALMOST SLUMPED THROUGH THE GROUND, I WAS SO SURPRISED TO KNOW WHO I WAS SUPPOSED TO BE. BUT THEN I HEARD A STEAMBOAT WHISTLE.

WHAT IF THE REAL TOM COMES IN ON THAT BOAT? I GOT TO HEAD HIM OFF.

I LEFT MY BAG ON THE WHARF. RECKON I'D BETTER GO TAKE THE WAGON AND FETCH IT.

I STARTED DOWN THE ROAD AND, SURE ENOUGH, THERE WAS TOM SAWYER.

YOU LOOK LIKE HUCK FINN, BUT HE WAS MURDERED. ARE--ARE YOU HIS GHOST?

HONEST INJUN, TOM, I AIN'T A GHOST.

WASN'T YOU EVER MURDERED AT ALL?

NO, BUT LISTEN HERE. I'M IN A REAL FIX NOW.

I TOLD HIM THE WHOLE STORY.

AND JIM IS HERE AND I JUST GOT TO STEAL HIM OUT OF SLAVERY.

I'LL HELP YOU. I'LL LET ON I'M MY BROTHER SID, COME FOR A VISIT, TOO.

SOON...

WE WEREN'T LOOKING FOR YOU TOO, SID, BUT UNCLE SILAS AND I ARE SURE GLAD TO HAVE YOU.

THAT EVENING...

HE'S TAKING VITTLES IN THE HUT, AND THERE'S A LOCK ON THE DOOR. JIM MUST BE IN THERE.

TOMORROW NIGHT WE CAN FETCH MY RAFT. THEN WE'LL STEAL THE KEY TO THE HUT AND SHOVE OFF DOWN THE RIVER ON THE RAFT WITH JIM. WOULDN'T THAT WORK?

WORK? LIKE RATS A-FIGHTING. BUT IT'S TOO BLAMED SIMPLE. LET'S LOOK AROUND.

THAT HOLE'S BIG ENOUGH FOR JIM TO GET THROUGH IF WE WRENCH OFF THE BOARD.

I SHOULD HOPE WE CAN DO SOMETHING MORE COMPLICATED THAN THAT!

WE GOT TO DO IT IN A WAY THAT WOULD MAKE JIM A FREE MAN, AND MAYBE GET US ALL KILLED BESIDES.

I KNOW! WE'LL DIG HIM OUT WITH CASE KNIVES.

CONFOUND IT, THAT'S FOOLISH, TOM.

YES, BUT IT'S THE RIGHT WAY. ONE OF THEM PRISONERS IN A DUNGEON IN FRANCE DUG HIMSELF OUT THAT WAY.

IT TOOK HIM THIRTY-SEVEN YEARS-AND HE COME OUT IN CHINA.

JIM DON'T KNOW NOBODY IN CHINA.

BUT IT WEREN'T NO USE TO ARGUE WITH TOM, SO THAT NIGHT WE STARTED.

THIS AIN'T NO THIRTY-SEVEN YEAR JOB. THIS IS A THIRTY-EIGHT YEAR JOB.

WELL, IT AIN'T MORAL AND IT AIN'T RIGHT, BUT I GUESS WE GOT TO DIG HIM OUT WITH PICKS AND LET ON IT'S CASE KNIVES.

NOW YOU'RE TALKING!

IN ABOUT TWO HOURS AND A HALF, THE JOB WAS DONE.

HUCK, CHILE, I'M GLAD TO SEE YOU! AND TOM, TOO!

AND WE GOT TO HAVE A BIG STONE TO SCRATCH AN INSCRIPTION ON--LIKE "HERE A CAPTIVE, HEART BUSTED."

THERE'S A GRINDSTONE DOWN BY THE MILL.

WE WENT DOWN TO FETCH IT, BUT.

WE CAN'T DO IT ALONE. WE'LL HAVE TO GET JIM.

WE SLID JIM'S CHAIN OFF THE BED LEG AND TOLD HIM TO COME WITH US.

JIM AND ME LAID INTO THAT GRINDSTONE AND GOT HER BACK TO THE HUT, WHILE TOM SUPERINTENDED. HE COULD OUT SUPERINTEND ANY BOY I EVER SEE. HE KNOWED HOW TO DO EVERYTHING.

WHEN WE GOT BACK TO THE HUT, WE HELPED JIM FIX HIS CHAIN BACK ON THE BED LEG. THEN ...

YOU GOT ANY SPIDERS IN HERE, JIM?

THANK GOODNESS, I AIN'T.

ALL RIGHT. WE'LL GET YOU SOME.

BUT, BLESS YOU, I DON'T WANT NONE. I'D JUST AS SOON HAVE A RATTLESNAKE.

NOW THAT'S A GOOD IDEA. WE'LL GET YOU A RATTLESNAKE, TOO. EVERY PRISONER'S GOT TO HAVE SOME KIND OF PET.

I AIN'T UNREASONABLE, BUT IF YOU FETCH A RATTLESNAKE IN HERE, I'M GOIN' TO LEAVE, THAT'S SURE.

WELL, THEN, WE'LL GET YOU SOME GARTER-SNAKES AND YOU CAN TIE BUTTONS TO THEIR TAILS.

I COULD GET ALONG WITHOUT THEM, TOO. I NEVER KNOWED IT WAS SO MUCH BOTHER TO BE A PRISONER.

THE NEXT MORNING...

NOW JIM NEEDS A ROPE LADDER.

WHAT DO HE WANT OF A ROPE LADDER WHEN WE'RE GOING TO SNEAK HIM OUT FROM UNDER THE CABIN?

IT'S IN THE REGULATIONS. ALL PRISONERS GOT TO HAVE A ROPE LADDER. WE'LL SEND IT TO HIM IN A PIE.

FIRST WE HAD TO BORROW A SHEET.

THEN WE TORE IT IN LITTLE STRINGS AND TWISTED THEM INTO A ROPE.

WE GOT ENOUGH HERE FOR FORTY PIES.

WE BAKED THE PIE IN UNCLE SILAS' ANTIQUE BRASS WARMING PAN.

THE PERSON THAT EATS THIS SHOULD FETCH A KEG OF TOOTHPICKS ALONG.

WE PUT THE PIE IN WITH JIM'S VITTLES.

WHAT THEY DOIN' TO ME NOW?

WE VISITED JIM AGAIN THAT NIGHT.

TRY TO RAISE A FLOWER IN HERE. AND WATER IT WITH YOUR TEARS.

SHE'LL DIE ON MY HANDS, SURE ENOUGH, BECAUSE I DON'T SCARCELY EVER CRY.

DO THE BEST YOU CAN WITH AN ONION.

A FEW DAYS LATER ...

WHAT ARE YOU DOING

WRITING A NONNAMOUS LETTER TO UNCLE SILAS. HE'S GETTING READY TO TURN JIM IN, SO WE HAVE TO ACT FAST. HOW'S THIS?

A DESPRATE GANG OF CUTTHROATS IS GOING TO STEAL YOUR RUNAWAY SLAVE TONIGHT.

UNKNOWN FRIEND

WHAT DO WE WANT TO WARN THEM FOR? LET THEM FIND IT OUT FOR THEMSELVES.

YOU CAN'T DEPEND ON THEM. IF WE DON'T GIVE THEM NOTICE, THIS ESCAPE WON'T AMOUNT TO NOTHING. IT WILL GO OFF PERFECTLY FLAT.

WHO'S GOING TO DELIVER THE LETTER?

IT'S GOT TO BE A SERVANT GIRL. YOU HOOK ONE OF THE GIRL'S DRESSES, PUT IT ON, AND SHOVE THE LETTER UNDER THE DOOR.

I COULD CARRY IT JUST AS HANDY IN MY OWN TOGS.

YOU WOULDN'T LOOK LIKE A SERVANT GIRL, THEN, WOULD YOU? AIN'T YOU GOT NO PRINCIPLES AT ALL?

WELL, I DONE IT, BUT I WASN'T HAPPY ABOUT IT.

THAT NIGHT...

EVERYTHING ALL SET FOR THE ESCAPE, HUCK?

YES, AS SOON AS I GO DOWN TO THE CELLAR TO SNITCH SOME BUTTER FOR OUR LUNCH. I'LL MEET YOU AT THE HUT.

I HAD JUST GOT THE BUTTER WHEN...

OH, OH. SOMEONE'S COMING.

I CLAPPED THE BUTTER UNDER MY HAT.

THEN...

WHAT ARE YOU DOING HERE THIS TIME OF NIGHT? YOU JUST MARCH UP TO THE SETTING ROOM AND STAY THERE TILL I COME.

MY, BUT THERE WAS A CROWD THERE!

TOM'S NONNAMOUS LETTER WORKED REAL GOOD. HALF THE COUNTRY'S HERE TO CATCH US.

NE WAS ALL RIGHT UNTIL TOM'S BRITCHES 'ATCHED ON A SPLINTER WHICH SNAPPED AND MADE A NOISE.

WHO'S THAT? ANSWER, OR I'LL SHOOT!

NE LIT OUT, AND THE BULLETS WHIZZED AROUND US.

NE MADE IT TO THE RAFT.

YOU'RE A FREE MAN AGAIN, JIM.

IT WAS DONE BEAUTIFUL-- MIXED UP AND SPLENDID.

AND I'VE GOT A BULLET IN MY LEG. AIN'T THAT GRAND?

Nobody said anything for a minute.

SAY IT, JIM.

I DON'T BUDGE A STEP WITHOUT A DOCTOR FOR TOM.

DON'T BE CRAZY!

NO, JIM'S RIGHT. I'M GOING FOR HELP.

I woke up a doctor and told him where the raft was.

YOU WAIT HERE.

I laid down to get some sleep. When I waked up, it was morning. I ran back to town.

UNCLE SILAS!

WHERE HAVE YOU BEEN?

I said that me and Sid were out looking for the runaway slave. I let on that Sid would be home soon. Later...

SID! HE'S BEEN HURT!

...E MEN WAS PRETTY MAD AT JIM.

LET'S HANG HIM.

THAT'LL TEACH SLAVES NOT TO RUN AWAY!

NOW, WAIT A MINUTE.

WHEN I GOT TO THE BOY, I FOUND I COULDN'T CUT THE BULLET OUT WITHOUT HELP. THIS MAN HELPED ME, AND HE WAS RISKING HIS FREEDOM TO DO IT. HE'S A GOOD MAN AND DESERVES KINDER TREATMENT.

LATER, TOM CAME TO.

DID YOU TELL AUNT SALLY HOW WE DID IT--SET JIM FREE?

MERCY SAKES! IT WAS YOU TWO?

BUT HE DIDN'T GET AWAY. HE'S LOCKED IN THE HUT AGAIN.

THEY CAN'T DO THAT! HE'S A FREE MAN! MISS WATSON DIED AND SET HIM FREE IN HER WILL. I DIDN'T LET ON BEFORE BECAUSE I WANTED TO HAVE SOME ADVENTURE OUT OF IT.

I'D A WADED NECK DEEP IN BLOOD TO--GOODNESS ALIVE, AUNT POLLY!

THERE SHE STOOD, TOM'S AUNT POLLY.

I LIT FOR COVER.

NOW WHAT HAVE YOU BEEN UP TO, TOM?

TOM? YOU MEAN SID.

NO, I MEAN TOM. THE OTHER RASCAL IS HUCK FINN. COME OUT FROM UNDER THAT BED, HUCK.

THEY WERE THE MOST MIXED-UPEST-LOOKING PERSONS I EVER SEE.

I JUST HAD TO LET AUNT SALLY THINK I WAS TOM.

WHEN I DIDN'T GET ANY ANSWER TO MY LETTERS, I CAME HERE TO FIND OUT WHAT WAS GOING ON.

I DIDN'T GET ANY LETTERS.

I BEEN KEEPING THEM FOR YOU. I THOUGHT THERE WEREN'T NO HURRY.

AS SOON AS EVERYTHING WAS EXPLAINED, THEY SET JIM FREE.

ERE'S $40 FOR BEING SUCH A OOD PRISONER, JIM.

BLESS YOU, I'M RICH!

NOW WE SHOULD ALL GET AN OUTFIT AND GO FOR HOWLING ADVENTURES IN INJUN TERRITORY.

I AIN'T GOT NO MONEY FOR TO BUY AN OUTFIT. I RECKON PAP'S COME BACK AND GOT ALL MY MONEY BY NOW.

HE AIN'T COMIN' BACK NO MORE, HUCK.

EMEMBER THAT DEAD MAN WE SAW N THE FLOATIN' HOUSE AFTER THE RAINSTORM? THAT WAS YOUR PAP.

THERE AIN'T NOTHING MORE TO WRITE ABOUT. AUNT POLLY IS TAKING TOM BACK HOME AND I RECKON I'LL LIGHT OUT FOR INJUN TERRITORY AHEAD OF THE REST. AUNT SALLY, SHE WANTS TO ADOPT ME AND CIVILIZE ME, AND I CAN'T STAND IT.

I BEEN THERE BEFORE.

THE END

ADVENTURES OF
HUCKLEBERRY FINN
MARK TWAIN

More than a century after publication, *Huck Finn* remains an essential American novel. Even Ernest Hemingway, positioning himself as the most important writer our country ever produced, noted that "all modern American literature comes from one book by Mark Twain called *Huckleberry Finn*." But the novel emerged in a hostile atmosphere. It was banned from one library upon publication and has been banned, burnt and censured constantly since then. But this story—about a barely literate river-rat on the verge of manhood, who tries uncertainly to help a slave to freedom as he searches for his own—just won't die. It's been rewritten dozens of times, made into many movies, and put on the Broadway stage.

It isn't a perfect book, but it is a great one, a work that captures in the character of Huck Finn our national ambivalence about race, about nature, about justice, and about our own "sivilization," as Huck calls it.

The Author

Samuel Langhorne Clemens, who was born in Missouri in 1835, began signing the name Mark Twain to his journalism in the Virginia City, Nevada *Territorial Enterprise*, in February of 1863. He had followed his older brother Orion into the printing trade, first with an apprenticeship when he was teenager, and later into Orion's series of unsuccessful print shops. Sam Clemens lucked into an opportunity to become a Mississippi River steamboat pilot, his childhood ambition; unfortunately, the Civil War ended his successful four-year run on the river. After a brief stint fighting for the Confederacy, Clemens traveled with Orion to Nevada, where President Abraham Lincoln had appointed Orion Clemens Territorial Secretary. Prospecting halfheartedly for a few months, Sam landed his job at the *Territorial Enterprise*, and began his career as Mark Twain, a career that soon encompassed not only newspapers, magazines and books, but the stage too, as Mark Twain became the nation's most popular comedian.

Mark Twain wrote *Adventures of Huckleberry Finn* over a period of eight years, starting in 1876. That was the year he published *The Adventures of Tom Sawyer*, the first novel he had written on his own. He had hoped that his first novel would sell as well as had his first two books of personal adventure, *Innocents Abroad* and *Roughing It*. Those two volumes, his lecture tours, and his marriage in 1870 to Olivia Langdon, a savvy and educated heiress, had brought Mark Twain popularity and affluence. But he wanted respect, too, and the Boston literary tastemakers respected novels. When his friend, Boston editor and writer William Dean Howells, championed *Tom Sawyer*, Twain started on *Huck Finn* as a sequel. He wrote Howells in 1876 that he had begun another boys' book, "more to be at work than anything else. I have written 400 pages on it—therefore it is very nearly half done. It is *Huck Finn's Autobiography*. I like it only tolerably well, as far as I have got, & may possibly pigeonhole or burn the MS when it is done."

He did not burn the manuscript, but he did put it aside, working on it sporadically until 1884. By then, many things had changed for Mark Twain, and for the man behind him, Samuel Langhorne Clemens. Twain had his first major success in 1865 with his short story "The Celebrated Jumping Frog of Calaveras County," and cemented his fame with a series of lecture tours. Mark Twain was a performance, the most successful on-going show of the post-Civil War American cultural landscape. By the mid-1880s, Sam Clemens wanted to take full control of Mark Twain's creative enterprises. He wanted to be his own publisher, and he wanted to produce his own lecture tour.

He was still not quite certain how the public would react to an artist dirtying his hands with the business of fame. He not only hired Charley Webster, his nephew-by-marriage, to run his publishing firm, but also called the firm Charles L. Webster & Company. And when Webster negotiated the contract for the lecture tour Clemens wanted Mark Twain to make in support of *Huck Finn*, he was working under strict instructions to make it look as the promoter was the force behind the campaign, not the author.

When the book came out, though, it did not sell as well as Clemens hoped. It did about as well as his earlier novels, but not nearly so well as his travel books. He went on tour with George Washington Cable, a New Orleans writer of novels of Creole life, as his opening act; Clemens chose Cable as Twain's stage mate because he was generally thought to be the most forward-thinking man in America on the subject of race-relations. By calling the tour "Twins of Genius," Clemens painted Mark Twain and his new book *Huck Finn* with the same brush, posing Twain as radically progressive about a subject that had tied white America in knots. *Adventures of Huckleberry Finn* became a lightning-rod for differing opinion on this divisive issue; a group outside Boston, Massachusetts played right into Clemens' hands. As he wrote to Charley Webster, "The Committee of the Public Library of Concord, Mass, have given us a rattling tip-top puff which will go into every paper in the country. They have expelled *Huck* from their library as 'trash and suitable only for the slums.' That will sell 25,000 copies for us sure."

Success brought Clemens more opportunities: he published the autobiography of Ulysses S. Grant, General of the Union Army during the War and later President of the United States. Clemens sold more than a quarter of a million copies of the two volume set, which made the Grant family, his publishing firm, and himself a pile of money. Unfortunately, the Grant book was Charley Webster's last achievement. He spent the publishing company into debt, which meant Clemens had to pour more money into it at a time when he had already gambled on a typesetting machine.

The machine and the publishing firm went bust around the same time. Bankrupt by the mid-1890's, Clemens had to take Mark Twain on a 'round-the-world tour in 1895-6 to earn back enough money to repay his creditors. His eldest daughter Susy died while he was on tour, shattering his family. His wife Livy never recovered from the loss, and died in 1904. Mark Twain rebounded after her death for a few years as the white-suited philosopher—the most photographed and most quoted man in the world. He fell ill in 1909, his health succumbing to the 40 cigars he smoked each day. Samuel Langhorne Clemens died on April 21, 1910.

Characters

Huckleberry Finn—the abandoned adolescent son of St. Petersburg's town drunk. After having saved the widow Douglas and found a fortune in gold at the end of *The Adventures of Tom Sawyer*, Huck has been adopted by the widow and her sister Miss Watson and is suffering through the process of being "sivilized."
This includes learning to read and write, which is why we have a book about his adventures.

Tom Sawyer—Huck's friend and leader of St. Petersburg's boys. His mind is full of adventure, mostly drawn from the fiction he reads. An orphan, Tom, along with his half-brother Sid, is being raised by his aunt Polly, his mother's sister.

Jim—Miss Watson's slave. Threatened with being sold away from his wife and two children, he runs off. He wants to reach the free states so he can earn enough money to buy his family out of bondage.

Pap—Huck's father, a violent drunk, and an unrepentant thief. He returns to town when he hears of Huck's good fortune and determines to exert his parental rights for the first time in his son's life.

The Grangerford Family—with whom Huck stays for a while. They fight a bloody and deadly feud with the Shepherdsons. Buck Grangerford is Huck's particular friend. Sophia is disloyal to the clan, in love with a Shepherdson youth.

The King—an elderly con artist working small towns along the southern Mississippi River.

The Duke—the same, only half the King's age.

The Wilks Family—the daughters of the recently deceased Peter Wilks's, an Englishman. The King and the Duke pretend to be Peter Wilks' lost brothers, in order to steal the girls' inheritance.

The Phelps Family—Tom Sawyer's relatives, on whose Arkansas plantation Jim is held captive after being sold by the King and the Duke.

also—**Judith Loftus**, a St. Petersburg woman; **Boggs**, a vocal drunk in Bricksville; **Colonel Sherburn**, the man who kills Boggs; **Peter Wilks'** doctor, who doubts the King and Duke; the **thieves** on the Walter Scott, a wrecked steamboat.

Plot

Adventures of Huckleberry Finn is an episodic story held together primarily by the voice of its young and delinquent narrator. Huck learned to read and write only between the end of *Tom Sawyer* and the beginning of his own book. He has no mother, and his drunken father frequently abandons him, but after his heroic behavior in *Tom Sawyer*, he is no longer the village pariah. As Huck explains, "The widow Douglas, she took me for her son, and allowed she would sivilize me; but it was rough living in the house all the time, considering how dismal regular and decent the widow was in all her ways." His desire to get back to his old ways—free from all obligations, sleeping in barrels and grubbing for food—kicks off the events of *Huck Finn*.

A Note on the Text

The version of *Adventures of Huckleberry Finn* you read may vary significantly from the version published during Mark Twain's life. The most likely difference is the inclusion in Chapter XVI of what has become known as "The Raftsmen's Passage," the game of boast and insult Huck hears from his hiding place on the raft, where he has gone for information. This passage was written for *Huck Finn* but was published instead in *Life on the Mississippi*, to fill out that book, which appeared two years earlier. Twain wanted to repeat the section in *Huck Finn*, but decided at the very end not to. Many versions today include these pages.

Even more variations entered the text in 1996. For most of this century, the first half of the manuscript of *Huck Finn* was missing. The second half was in the possession of the Buffalo Public Library, in New York, and a letter indicated that Twain had also sent the first half to a man named James Gluck, who had solicited the manuscript for the library's collection. The manuscript turned up in California in 1991 when Gluck's granddaughters were cleaning out their attic. Gluck had the manuscript in his possession when he died. It was put in the trunk with the rest of his papers and not opened for almost 100 years. The manuscript showed that there were several more last-minute cuts and changes, including one story Jim tells about a cadaver and another comic scene at the tent revival. These have been added to at least one recent edition and might appear in the version you are reading.

Part the First, Chapters I-V *in which we meet Huckleberry Finn.*

"You don't know about me, without you have read a book by the name of 'The Adventures of Tom Sawyer,'" Huck says at the beginning of his book. "That book was made by Mr. Mark Twain, and he told the truth, mainly. There was things which he stretched, but mainly he told the truth. That is nothing. I never seen anybody but lied, one time or another." In the very first paragraph of the book, Huck invites the reader to ask what Huck is lying about; no reader will find it an easy question to answer.

Huck's heroism in *Tom Sawyer* has landed him in the house of the widow

Douglas and her sister Miss Watson, whom Huck called "a tolerable slim old maid". The prayers, the fancy food, the endless drilling in reading and in the Bible, and Huck's new, starchy clothes depress Huck. He notes, "I set down in a chair by the window and tried to think of something cheerful, but it warn't no use. I felt so lonesome I most wished I was dead." Only Tom Sawyer's midnight call— "me-yow! me-yow!"—relieves Huck. He scampers out the window and into the night with Tom Sawyer. who has

decided to found a Gang, whose business he describes as "Nothing only robbery and murder." This havoc can only be performed according to the strictest rules, as set down in the books of adventure Tom likes to read.

The months go peacefully by. "The longer I went to school the easier it got to be," Huck writes. "I was getting sort of used to the widow's ways, too, and they warn't so raspy on me." Then one morning Huck accidentally spills salt, and before he can toss some over his shoulder to ward off bad luck, Miss Watson cleans up the mess. Fearful of a change in his fortune, Huck goes outside and in the new-fallen snow he sees boot-tracks with a cross marked in the left heel. "I was up in a second and shinning down the hill" to Judge Thatcher's house. Huck insists that the Judge take Huck's half of the treasure he and Tom had found at the end of Tom Sawyer. Then he goes to "Miss Watson's nigger, Jim" to ask him to use his special powers of divination to read his future. When Huck "went up to his room that night, there set pap, his own self."

Huck has not seen his father for more than a year, and Mark Twain makes it clear that Huck was happy about the absence. "I'll take you down a peg before I get done with you," Pap threatens. "You're educated, too, they say; can read and write. You think you're better than your father, now, don't you, because he can't? Who told you you might meddle with such hifalut'n foolishness, hey?" After a few weeks of getting wildly drunk, making life miserable for Huck, and frustrating attempts by the widow and Judge Thatcher to terminate Pap Finn's parental rights, Huck's father snatches the boy and takes him to "an old log hut in a place where the timber was so thick you couldn't find it if you didn't know where it was."

Part the Second, Chapters VI-XVI
in which Huck escapes and find another escapee

Though Huck revels in his return to less civilized ways, he is a prisoner of his father, who locks him in the cabin, sometimes for several days, when he goes off on a drinking jag. Other times something in town so enrages him that he frightens Huck. "Call this a govment! why, just look at it and see what it's like," Pap rails after seeing a free Negro. "He had a gold watch and a chain, and a silver-headed cane—the awfulest old gray-headed nabob in the State. And what do you think? they said he was a p'fessor in a college, and could talk all kinds of languages, and knowed everything. And that ain't the wust. They said he could vote, when he was at home." Sometimes the liquor makes him hallucinate that Huck is the Angel of Death. After six months, "pap got too handy with his hick'ry"—that is, beat Huck with a

stick—and the boy decides to leave. When Pap goes on a bender, Huck cuts a hole in the side of the cabin and runs, making it look as if he's been murdered. "I did wish Tom Sawyer was there, I knowed he would take an interest in this kind of business, and throw in the fancy touches." He pushes off for Jackson's Island.

Huck spends three blissful days on Jackson's Island before discovering that he is not alone. Miss Watson's slave Jim, who escaped in the hubbub surrounding news of Huck Finn's "murder," has also chosen Jackson's Island as a hideout, to stay close to his wife and children, from whom he fears he will be separated. "I hear ole missus tell de widder she gwyne to sell me down to Orleans, but she didn' want to, but she could git eight hund'd dollars for me." He wants to head north to freedom and earn enough money to buy his family out of slavery.

Huck and Jim decide to help each other, for a while at least. They set up camp together and go scavenging in an old frame house they find floating down the rising river. Jim discovers a naked body inside, "shot in de back. I

reck'n he's ben dead two er three days," Jim cautioned Huck. "Doan' look at his face—it's too gashly." Later, Jim tells Huck that talking about the murdered man would bring bad luck, but Huck points out that they found eight dollars sewed into the lining of some clothes they took from the house. But bad luck does come when Huck plays a joke on Jim, placing a dead rattlesnake in his bedroll. The snake's mate bites Jim; it takes him more than a week to recover. By then, Huck feels "it was getting slow and dull, and I wanted to get a stirring up, some way." He decides to go into town to get the news; Jim dresses him like a girl in some of their found clothes, so no one will recognize him. He

BUT SHE COME SMASHING STRAIGHT THROUGH THE RAFT.

"Sometimes I lifted a chicken that warn't roosting comfortable," Huck explains. "Pap always said, take a chicken when you get a chance, because if you don't want him yourself you can easy find somebody that does, and a good deed ain't never forgot." When Huck persuades Jim to board a wrecked steamboat, they discover that a real band of robbers is using the boat as a hideout, and plan to kill one of their number. In a close escape, Huck and Jim take the thieves' boat. Huck worries that the wreck will sink before long and kill the lot, so he finds a man ashore and spins a tale of a lost family, with enough reward implied to induce the man

meets a Miss Judith Loftus, who quickly sees that he's a boy, but thinks he's a runaway apprentice. She also gives him the news of the town: that her husband is headed to Jackson's Island later that night to hunt for Jim. Huck scampers back to camp, shouting, "Git up and hump yourself, Jim! There ain't a minute to lose. They're after us!"

The two fugitives float off down river on a raft, traveling by night.

go over to the wreck. Feeling virtuous, he writes that "I wished the widow knowed about it. I judged she would be proud of me for helping these rapscallion, because rapscallions and dead beat is the kind the widow and good people takes the most interest in." Huck rejoins Jim and they head for Cairo, Illinois, where the Ohio River joins the Mississippi, aiming to follow the Ohio to the free states.

But the night they expect to pass Cairo, a fog engulfs them. Huck in the canoe and Jim on the raft become separated and seemingly lost to one another, especially as the weather worsens. After the storm, Huck finds the raft at last. Jim holds the rudder in his sleep. Huck climbs aboard and wakes him, pretending that Jim dreamed the fog and storm, and that they'd never been separated. Jim falls for Huck's trick until Huck points out the mess the storm left on the raft. Jim replies, "Dat truck dah is trash; en trash is what people is dat puts dirt on de head er dey fren's en makes 'em ashamed." Huck writes, "It was fifteen minutes before I could work myself up to go and humble myself to a nigger—but I done it, and I warn't ever sorry for it afterward, neither".

Before long, the two get into another scrape, even more serious than the fog. A steamboat runs over their raft. Huck and Jim are separated for real. Huck paddles to shore and straight into worse trouble.

Part the Third, Chapters XVII-XVIII *in which Huck find himself in the middle of a feud*

In these chapters (omitted from the Classics Illustrated adaptation) Huck makes his way to a nearby house, where he is greeted at gun point. Even Buck Grangerford, who is Huck's age, "thirteen or fourteen or along there," comes in with his gun. The Grangerford home is filled with all the trappings of gentry, but despite their formal refinement, they remain on constant watch for their rivals, the Shepherdsons. One day, near the steamboat landing the families share, Buck rushes Huck into hiding and

then shoots at Harney Shepherdson, passing by on horseback. It's a feud, Buck explains. This one has been going on for thirty years, following a murder by a man who came up short on a lawsuit. "By and by everybody's killed off, and there ain't no more feud," Buck tells Huck. "But it's kind of slow, and takes a long time."

Huck unknowingly worsens the feud when he retrieves Sophia Grangerford's Bible for her. The Bible contains a message in it, mentioning a time. He can't think of what else to do, so he delivers it. Meanwhile, one of the Grangerford slaves tempts Huck to a sheltered spot, where he finds Jim. The raft is all right, and the two are ready to leave again, except Huck wants to say his good-byes to his new friend Buck first. The next morning,

however, something has gone wrong. Sophia Grangerford and Harney Shepherdson eloped at the time assigned on the message Huck delivered. All-out war has begun. Huck finds Buck and a cousin hiding behind a woodpile. "He said his father and his two brothers was killed, and two or three of the enemy." But while Huck watches, the Shepherdson clan surprises the Grangerford boys and chases them into the river. "The men run along the bank shooting at them and singing out, 'Kill them, kill them!'" Huck concludes, "I wished I hadn't come ashore that night, to see such things. I ain't ever going to get shut of them—lots of times I dream about them."

Part the Fourth, Chapters XIX-XXIV *in which Huck and Jim befriend royalty*

After the feud, the raft is a relief to Huck. "Other place do seem so cramped up and smothery, but a raft don't. You feel mighty free and easy and comfortable on a raft." He and Jim go back to running nights and sleeping days. Except for the fact that they have overshot Cairo and now have no idea where they are going or what they are doing, they feel better; at least they are together. Their comfort doesn't last long.

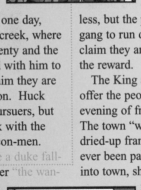

Looking for adventure one day, Huck takes a canoe up a creek, where two men—one about seventy and the other about thirty—plead with him to save their lives. They claim they are being chased for no reason. Huck helps them shake their pursuers, but then he and Jim are stuck with the two, who turn out to be con-men. The younger claims to be a duke fallen on hard times, the older "the wanderin', exiled, trampled-on and sufferin' rightful King of France": Huck has to think fast to invent a story about himself and Jim these old scam artists will believe.

Before long the King and the Duke "allowed they would 'lay out a campaign,' as they called it. The duke went down into his carpet-bag

and fetched up a lot of printed bills." In one he is a lecturer on phrenology, in another an expert at finding water and gold, in another a famous actor. He convinces the King to perform with him, for the small towns along the way. In one town the Duke "borrows" a printing press on which he sets a poster offering a $200 reward for a runaway slave who looks just like Jim. Meanwhile the King attends a tent revival, where he announces to the crowd that he had been a pirate until this camp meeting reformed him. Moved by his spiritual redemption, the people toss money into his hat. The King returns to the raft with almost a hundred dollars. The duke has taken in much less, but the poster will allow the gang to run during the day; they will claim they are taking Jim south for the reward.

The King and the Duke plan to offer the people of Bricksville an evening of fractured Shakespeare. The town "was most all old shackly dried-up frame concerns that hadn't ever been painted." A drunk rides into town, shouting insults against a man named Sherburn. Sherburn patiently gives him until one o'clock to stop, but the drunk misses his deadline. Sherburn steps out into the street and shoots him twice, point blank. "Colonel Sherburn he tossed his pistol onto the ground, and turned around on his heels and walked off." A mob gathers to lynch Sherburn, sweeping Huck along with them as they swarm to his house. When Sherburn steps onto his roof with a gun in his hand, the gang falls silent. "If any lynching's going to be done, it will be done in the dark, southern fashion," Sherburn berates them. "When they come, they'll bring their masks, and fetch a man along. Now leave." The mob disperses. Huck sneaks off to go see a circus.

The Duke and the King fail to draw a crowd with the Shakespeare, so they advertise a risqué show: "LADIES AND CHILDREN NOT ADMITTED." The Duke says, "If that line don't fetch them, I don't know Arkansaw!" They skin the crowd for two nights, then skip town, expecting retribution on the third. The King and Duke drink to the success of their scam. Jim asks Huck, "Don't it sprise you, de way dem kings carries on?" Huck answers, "All kings is mostly rapscallions, as fur as I can make out." And before long the rapscallion King enlists the Duke in another con.

Part the Fifth, Chapters XXV-XXX
in which Huck shows his true colors
The King and Duke decide to play the bereaved English brothers of the wealthy Mississippian Peter Wilks: William, the younger, is deaf and dumb; Harvey, the elder, is a minister. They arrive just too late to appear at Wilks's deathbed, and the inhabitants of the town sympathetically greet them with the bad news. The King, as Harvey, begins to wail and then signs to the Duke, as William, who joins in. "If they warn't the beatenest lot, them two frauds," Huck remarks.

"If I ever struck anything like it, I'm a nigger. It was enough to make a body ashamed of the human race."

Peter Wilks has left his brothers his three teenage daughters—Mary Jane, Joanna and Susan—and cash and assets worth almost twenty thousand dollars. The King and the Duke make a show of giving it all to the daughters, to defeat any suspicion that they might not be who they claim. Peter's friend, the town doctor, doubts the brothers, but the daughters entrust the frauds with the money, which they hide for their getaway. Huck plays the brothers' servant— badly, since he knows nothing about life in England—while Jim, now dressed as a sick Arab, guards the raft.

First the con-men sell off Peter Wilks' property, promising to take the Wilks girls home with them to England. But as Huck gets to know Joanna, Susan and especially Mary Jane, he feels sorry for them. He steals the money from the King and Duke, hiding it in the dead man's casket, which is awaiting burial. Against the Duke's advice, the King presses ahead with the sale of Peter Wilks' property, including his slaves. This sale breaks apart one slave family, which breaks Mary Jane's heart. Huck comforts her by confessing the scam; armed with knowledge of the fraud, Mary Jane disappears just as two more con-artists, also posing as Wilks's brothers, arrive in town to play the same scam. The townspeople hold an open inquest, and the King and Duke are exposed as frauds. As a final test, the people question all four of the humbugs about a tattoo on the dead man's chest. When no one can agree what the tattoo says, the group decides to dig up the body.

In the hubbub after finding the bag of gold in the casket, Huck runs to the raft. "Out with you Jim, and set her loose!" he calls out. "Glory be to goodness, we're shut of them!" But as soon as they float clear, they see the King and the Duke bearing down on them in a skiff. "Tryin' to give us the slip, was ye, you pup! Tired of our company—hey?" The Duke and the King accuse one another of stealing the money, fight, and then go off and get drunk together. Before a few days pass, they "begun to lay their heads together in the wigwam and talk low and confidential two or three hours at a time. Jim and me got uneasy".

Part the Sixth, Chapters XXXI-the Last *in which Huck's true colors fade*

The King and the Duke, now penniless, liquidate their only asset. They send Huck off on an errand and, using the false reward poster, they sell their rights to Jim for forty dollars. When Huck returns to the raft, he finds it deserted. "I thought, 'til I wore my head sore, but I couldn't see no way out of the trouble," Huck mourns. He decides that "it would be a thousand times better for Jim to be a slave at home where his family was, as long as he's got to be a slave." So he writes a letter to Miss Watson, telling her

where Jim is. He tries to pray, but finds he can't. His head is full of all the kindnesses and friendship Jim has shown him, and full of sympathy for a man who loved his family so deeply that he threw himself in with someone as lowly as Huck in order to get them back. Huck decides that if turning Jim in was good, he would rather go to hell. "It was awful thoughts, and awful words, but they was said. And I let them stay said, and never thought no more about reforming," Huck states. "And for a starter, I would go to work and steal Jim out of slavery again; and if I could think up anything worse, I would do that, too."

Jim has been sold to Silas and Sally Phelps, so Huck goes to their farm. He receives a traveler's welcome, because the Phelpses are expecting a visit from their young nephew Tom Sawyer, and they all assume Huck is Tom. Now Huck is on steady ground: he can play Tom Sawyer easily. His only concern is that the real Tom will show up—as he does. Huck gets to Tom before the Phelpses do. Tom thinks the whole plan is great fun and pretends to be his own brother Sid, coming along to Arkansas as a surprise.

Huck wants to free Jim and get away as quickly a possible, but Tom has his own ideas. He's read books about daring escapes, and he wants Jim's escape to follow the model he's gathered from his reading. Tom tells Huck his plan, "and I see in a minute it was worth fifteen of mine, for style, and would make Jim as free a man as mine would, and maybe get us all killed besides." Huck is bothered that Tom, with all his intelligence and respectability, "was actually going to help steal that nigger out of slavery." With Tom willing to risk shame for himself, Huck doesn't feel he can object to any detail of Tom's plan, cruel as it might be to Jim.

Tom's plan includes a note alerting the Phelpses of the secret plan to steal him out of slavery. The neighbors, fully armed, come to protect the Phelps's property. Tom, Huck and Jim slip off into the night and make it to the raft, but not before Tom is shot in the leg by their pursuers. Tom is all ready to shove off, but Huck and Jim won't go until they've had a doctor look at Tom's leg. Huck goes for the physician, and then returns to the farm. It isn't until the next morning that Tom is carried back to the Phelps's house, accompanied by the doctor, Jim and a group of men. Tom is out of his head with pain, and Jim is silent beside him. The men "cussed Jim considerble, though, and give him a cuff or two, side the head, once in a while, but Jim never said nothing, and he never let on to know me." After the doctor speaks in Jim's defense he is more gently treated, but he is still a slave, and in captivity.

When Tom returns to his senses, he thinks the plan succeeded. "He was so proud and joyful, he just couldn't hold it in, and his tongue just went it." But when Sally lets him know that Jim is locked up again, Tom "rose square up in bed, with his eye hot, and his nostrils opening and shutting like gills, and sings out to me: 'They hain't no right to shut him up! Shove!—and don't you lose a minute. Turn him loose! he ain't no slave, he's as free as any cretur that walks this earth!'" Miss Watson has died since Jim and Huck left St. Petersburg, freeing Jim in her will. Tom had helped to liberate Jim only because he was already free.

Just then, Tom's aunt Polly strolls in, having made the trip to Arkansas because of her sister Sally's letters about Tom and Sid. The identities of the boys are straightened out, and Tom pays Jim forty dollars for being so good a prisoner in his game of escape. Tom wants Huck to "go for howling adventures amongst the Injuns, over in the Territory, for a couple of weeks or two; and I says, all right, that suits me, but I ain't got no money for to buy the outfit." Tom reminds him of his fortune back home, money Huck thought his father has drunk away by this time. But Jim breaks the news that the "gashly" body in the house they found floating near Jackson's Island was Huck's pap. Huck decides to "light out for the Territory ahead of the rest."

The depth of *Huck Finn* makes the novel great. It isn't only that the book handles its subject matter with elegance, authority and power, but that the novel covers many important issues without losing its focus on Huck Finn and his troubles coping with a dishonest world. The following paragraphs touch on only some of the themes Mark Twain explored in his book. They are not separate issues; rather, they are all interwoven into the texture of the novel.

RACE

No matter what anyone tells you, *Huck Finn* is not a racist book, except in the way that any acknowledgment of race is racist. Mark Twain used the word 'nigger' because it was the term used by the people he depicts to indicate a person with African ancestral roots. Huck Finn is racist, but he is less racist than the other people in the book, and he is willing to learn how not to be. It is his education in the fundamental virtues of people that drives his relationship with Jim. And even though Huck comes to appreciate Jim's humanity, he never entirely believes that slavery is wrong. When he decides to steal Jim out of slavery toward the end of the novel, he does it knowing that it is a bad thing to do. He cannot overcome his own training or his belief in the rightness of law, even if the law is immoral. This is a conflict Mark Twain had already dealt with—history had resolved it through the movement to abolish slavery and the war fought to accomplish that end. Twain uses irony—the distance between written words and their meaning—to show that although Huck is the least racist white

person in the book, Twain is himself far less racist than that. It has been said that Huck's language is based on the speech of a black boy Mark Twain met; in any case, the book works only because Huck occupies a place between Jim's world and the white one that pursues him. Perhaps what makes race in *Huck Finn* so controversial a topic is the vital anti-racism embodied in Huck himself.

SAVAGE AND 'SIVILIZED'

Huck lives on the line between a savage world and a civilized one, just as in the early 1800s, the time of this novel, the Mississippi River was the boundary between "civilized" white America and "savage" Indian America. In *Huck Finn* it is not clear which world is the better one. Huck constantly tries to escape the yoke of civilization, but once he is in the savage world he cannot wait to get back to civilization and see what is happening. Whenever he is bored on the river, he goes into town; he revels in the circus; he delights in gossip. In fact, the civilized world is actually more barbaric than the savage one. For example, it takes a long history of civilization to create a feud like the one between the Grangerfords and the Shepherdsons. The King and the Duke represent civilization at its highest and most corrupt level. Huck's uncertain feelings about which world to choose reflect the ambiguity with which Twain portrays them.

NATURE AND THE HUMAN SPIRIT

Huck's descriptions of the natural world often interrupt the flow of the novel's narrative. The peacefulness of the river, the eeriness of the fog, the awesome power of a storm, the deep loneliness of a country morning are all tellingly revealed in Huck's sensitive account. No matter what horror he witnesses, the river and its surrounding land seem to restore his faith—but his faith in what? In his travels on the river, Huck witnesses several murders. He sees petty thievery and grand larceny. He watches both the sloth of the river town men and the pointless wild activity of Tom Sawyer. Can humans achieve the kind of spiritual peace Huck sees in the natural world? *Huck Finn* offers contradictory implications.

AUTHORITY

Huck is an adolescent, and that may explain everything: he hates authority. But in *Huck Finn*, the issue is not quite so simple. The morality of power relationships seems to constantly change: Huck knows that the King and the Duke are frauds, yet he calls them 'your majesty' and 'your grace,' and obeys them even when he cannot stomach them. Tom Sawyer can command Huck to do foolish and even cruel things. Good-hearted aunt Sally has no authority at all. The novel seems to imply that all authority is corrupt, yet the wisest men in the book are people of authority. Peter Wilks's doctor and the physician who removes the bullet from Tom's leg, Colonel Sherburn, and Judge Thatcher are all good and wise men, most of whom could have just as easily been tailors or shopkeepers as titled authorities. In Twain's world, power has a very ill-defined quality, except in the case of race, where even the lowliest white man lords it over a black one. Power relations remain unpredictable, but one fact remains: people in Huck's world use their power to kill and steal, often without punishment.

HISTORY

History is a hidden force in this book. Huck and Jim hide out on Jackson's Island: in fact, the action of the novel takes place during the years when Andrew Jackson or his successors occupied the White House. To Twain, Jacksonian America was like an idyll of democracy—except for the existence of slavery. But it is slavery that eroded the Jacksonian ideal and nearly destroyed the nation founded on it. Mark Twain wrote *Huck Finn* more than a decade after the Civil War, when the central problem of the novel—getting Jim to freedom—was no longer an issue: Jim is going to be free anyway, so why fret over his freedom? Twain grapples with that very problem in the ill-fitting final section of the book, when Tom allows Huck to go to enormous trouble just to "set a free nigger free." Huck's attempt to be a hero, his willingness to go to hell rather than let Jim languish in slavery, is defeated by the flow of history itself. In Huck's empty effort on Jim's behalf, Mark Twain implies that heroism is the servant of history, and not the other way around.

FOLK CULTURE AND WRITTEN CULTURE

This theme is repeated throughout *Adventures of Huckleberry Finn*. Tom Sawyer's world is defined by elaborate written stories. It is a bookish universe. Huck Finn, on the other hand, has only recently learned to read. His book reads like spoken English, a point Mark Twain makes in his explanatory note at the beginning of the text. Throughout *Huck Finn*, the written word plays an important and often destructive role. The note from Harney Shepherdson to Sophia Grangerford; the false runaway-slave poster; Tom Sawyer's precious tales of adventure—all these and more have dire results for Huck and the people he cares about. One reason for the division between the oral world of Huck and the written world of Tom is Huck's stature as a mythic hero: Huck undergoes a death and rebirth and becomes capable of assuming new identities at will. Huck tries to defeat the civilized world by freeing of one of its slaves. His failure to do so—Jim is free, but not through Huck's actions, and Huck ends the book as he begins it, running from the trap of civilization—can be blamed on the written word. Writing creates history; history is what freed Jim and the millions like him. But Huck, and other legendary heroes, live in a timeless world where nothing ever changes. This theme uncovers a sad and difficult problem: a written culture can't support mythic heroes like Huck Finn, who could not even free one able-bodied man from bondage. History needs writing to exist, but once it comes into being, it is more powerful than myth.

Study Questions

• Who would you rather be: Huck, Tom, or Jim? Why?

• *Adventures of Huckleberry Finn* has been banned from schools and libraries regularly since its first publication. What are the arguments for banning *Huck Finn*? Do you consider that they're valid? Is there an age at which someone is too young to read the novel?

• Mark Twain said that the Southern notion of "the awful sacredness of slave property" showed how easily early training could silence conscience. Do you think this is true? Does it explain why Huck worries "til I wore my head sore," about whether to write Miss Watson about Jim's whereabouts at the Phelps' farm?

• Is the portrait of Jim a fair one? Is it racist?

• Crosses, Bibles, prayers and religious gatherings occur frequently in *Huck Finn.* What is the role of religion in the novel?

• If Mark Twain wanted to introduce criminals into his narrative, why choose confidence men? Would their function be served as well if they were a pair of pickpockets? Murderers?

• What becomes of Huck after the close of the novel? Why does he go to the Territory? Is the Territory the best place for him?

About the Essayist:

Andrew Jay Hoffman is the author of *Inventing Mark Twain*, a biography of Samuel Langhorne Clemens; *Beehive*: a novel; and *Twain's Heroes, Twain's Worlds*. A Visiting Scholar at Brown University, he holds a Ph.D. in Literature from Brown University.